# Houndsley
## and
# Catina
### and Cousin Wagster

# Houndsley
## and
# Catina
## and Cousin Wagster

James Howe

*illustrated by* Marie-Louise Gay

CANDLEWICK PRESS

To Marie-Louise,
for your razzle and your dazzle—
and to Mark, you old dog, you!
J. H.

To Jim and Mark
M.-L. G.

Text copyright © 2018 by James Howe
Illustrations copyright © 2018 by Marie-Louise Gay

Candlewick Sparks®. Candlewick Sparks is a registered trademark of Candlewick Press, Inc.

First paperback edition in this format 2020

Library of Congress Catalog Card Number 2018956982
ISBN 978-0-7636-4709-4 (hardcover)
ISBN 978-1-5362-1599-1 (paperback)

20 21 22 23 24 25 LEO 10 9 8 7 6 5 4 3 2 1

Printed in Heshan, Guangdong, China

This book was typeset in Galliard and Tree-Boxelder.
The illustrations were done in watercolor, pencil, and collage.

Candlewick Press
99 Dover Street
Somerville, Massachusetts 02144

visit us at www.candlewick.com

# Contents

# Chapter One
# Cousin Wagster

The five o'clock train was right on time.

"I can hardly wait to meet your cousin Wagster," Catina said to Houndsley. "Is he a lot like you?"

"Not exactly," Houndsley replied in his soft-as-a-rose-petal voice. "He's much more . . ."

"HOUNDSLEY, YOU OLD DOG, YOU!" a voice bellowed from the distance.

"Let's just say he's much *more*," Houndsley said as he waved to his cousin.

HOUNDSLEY!

"Grand to see you, Hounds!" Cousin Wagster barked. "Splendid trip! Rip-roaring train! No end to the fun! And who is this? Wait, do not tell me! Why, this lovely vision in whiskers and fur must be Catina!"

Catina blushed. It had been a long time since anyone had called her a vision in whiskers and fur. In fact, she was quite sure no one had ever called her a vision in whiskers and fur.

"I've heard so much about you!" Wagster boomed. "Cousin Houndsley's best friend!"

"And I've heard so much about you," Catina said. "Houndsley's cousin who travels all over the world. That must be so exciting."

"It is, pretty lady, it is!"

Wagster took Catina by the arm and walked away, leaving Houndsley to carry his bags. Houndsley did not mind. He was very happy to see his cousin.

"Life is full of adventures just waiting to be had!" Wagster exclaimed. "Why, just look at me! Here I am, visiting Houndsley and meeting you! Another adventure! Isn't that grand? The world is one big razzle-dazzle, I tell you. It is one big razzle-dazzle!"

"All aboard!" the train conductor shouted.

There was so much noise that Houndsley could not hear what Wagster was saying now. But he could tell by the way Catina tilted her head and laughed that she found Cousin Wagster charming.

Everyone found Cousin Wagster charming.

Suddenly, Houndsley felt invisible.

# Chapter Two
# Good at Everything

That night, Houndsley invited Bert to join them for dinner.

"Are you making your famous three-bean chili?" Bert asked.

"No," Houndsley replied. "I am making Wagster's favorites: watermelon soup, macaroni and cheese, and artichoke fritters."

"Oh, that will be delicious," Bert said. "What will we have for dessert?"

Houndsley frowned. "I was going to make key-lime pie with whipped cream. But Cousin Wagster said that he will make dessert."

"Oh," said Bert. "Well, that's nice, but I doubt it will be as good as your key-lime pie with whipped cream."

But when he tasted Cousin Wagster's brownie crumble with butterscotch sauce, Bert exclaimed, "Oh, my! This is even better than your key-lime pie with whipped cream, Houndsley. Oh! I mean, that is to say, I . . ."

"Yes, yes," said Catina. "It's delicious, but . . ."

"Thank you!" Cousin Wagster said. Houndsley got up from the table, leaving his dessert unfinished.

After dinner, Cousin Wagster and

Catina beat Houndsley and Bert at

Ping-Pong, seven games in a row.

"That was buckets of fun!" Wagster

shouted. "What's next?"

Houndsley wanted to say that it was time for bed, but Cousin Wagster was soon doing card tricks and telling jokes and making everyone laugh with imitations of famous movie stars.

Catina and Bert clapped and laughed and said, "How do you do it?" and "That's amazing!" Houndsley grew quieter and quieter and quieter.

The next day, watching Wagster do a one-handed cartwheel, Catina whispered in Houndsley's ear, "Your cousin is good at everything."

Houndsley did not know what to say. It was true. Cousin Wagster was good at everything.

"We must ask him to come with us to our dance lesson tonight," Catina said.

"Oh," said Houndsley. Before he could say anything more, Catina ran to Wagster and asked him.

"Dance lesson? Jolly good fun!" Wagster bellowed. "We'll kick up our heels and dance the night away!"

A bird landed softly on a bush next to
Houndsley and chirped. Houndsley sighed.

"Oh, but wait," Cousin Wagster said.
"On second thought, I think I will stay
at home tonight and catch up on my
knitting."

"Oh, do you knit?" Catina asked.

"I love to knit!" Wagster cried.

"So do I!" said Catina.

She and Wagster talked excitedly about knitting while Houndsley packed up the picnic basket.

He thought about his dance lesson with Catina and smiled. At last, he would be able to do something he loved to do—something he was good at—and Cousin Wagster would not be there to do it better.

## Chapter Three
# Razzle~Dazzle

1 - 2 - 3 - 4          5 - 6 - 7 - 8

"The Lindy Hop has eight steps," Mimi,

the dancing teacher, called out. "Now,

follow me, everyone! And-a-one-two-

three-four-five-six-seven-eight!"

Houndsley had never had so much trouble learning a dance before. The problem was not that the steps were too hard. The problem was that Catina would not stop talking about Cousin Wagster.

"He is so much fun, isn't he?" Catina was saying. "And the way he makes everyone laugh! It's too bad that he has to leave tomorrow, isn't it? Houndsley? Ouch!"

"Oh, I am sorry, Catina," Houndsley said. "I didn't mean to step on your foot."

"Of course you didn't," said Catina. "But something is wrong. What is it?"

Mimi blew her whistle. "Let's take a break!" she called out.

Outside, Houndsley told Catina the truth.

"You keep talking about Cousin Wagster. How much fun he is. How he makes everyone laugh. How he is good at everything he does. I am afraid you like him more than you like me."

"Oh, my," Catina said. "I am sorry I have made you feel that way, Houndsley.

You are my best friend. You will be my best
friend forever. Cousin Wagster is like a
beautiful butterfly that appears in your
garden and makes your world brighter.
But then one day he flies off to brighten
someone else's garden."

"And I am like a moth," said
Houndsley.

Catina laughed. "Don't be silly," she
said. "You are like a beautiful butterfly that
*stays* in the garden. You make every day
brighter just by being you."

Houndsley blushed as Catina gave him a big hug.

"Break's over!" they heard Mimi cry.

"And by the way," said Catina, "your key-lime pie is much better than Wagster's brownie crumble."

The next morning, Houndsley and
Catina said good-bye to Cousin Wagster.
"What a grand time I've had!" Cousin
Wagster shouted. "Grander than grand!"

He thrust a package into Houndsley's
hands and said, "I made a little something
for the two of you."

"Oh, you shouldn't have," said Houndsley.

"Nonsense!" Cousin Wagster boomed. "It is my way of saying thank you for showing me such a good time. And now I am off to see the world and all its razzle-dazzle!"

After the train was out of sight,
Houndsley opened the package and took
out two knitted caps.

"Oh, dear," said Catina. "I guess Cousin Wagster isn't good at everything, after all."

"No," Houndsley said. "But he has a good heart. And that's what matters most."

Houndsley and Catina looked at each
other in their lopsided caps. They started
to laugh.

And then they walked back to the
quiet little corner of the world they called
home. It had all the razzle-dazzle they
could ever want.